Charles' Grand Adventure

Created by
Ali Webster and
Amy Meredith

Illustrated by
Avril Taberner

How many **red bow ties**
can you spot in the story?

Charles the Bear and his family are off on a trip;
they pack holiday clothes to wear on the ship.

It's exciting to sail off to **faraway** places;
to make some new friends and see lots of new faces.

CHARLES 1

TO THE
HARBOUR

The Prince's Trust believes that every young person should have the chance to succeed, helping 11 to 30-year-olds get into jobs, education and training. Many of the young people they help are in or are leaving care, facing issues such as homelessness or mental health problems, or have been in trouble with the law.

Million Makers is The Prince's Trust flagship entrepreneurial competition, where teams are challenged to turn an initial investment of £1,500 into at least £10,000 profit. The competition raises £1million annually for The Trust across the UK to support disadvantaged young people.

Team Cunard is a group of professionals from Cunard who are excited to be part of this challenge, publishing this book as part of their fundraising efforts.

By purchasing this book, and sharing *Charles' Grand Adventure*, you are changing lives; supporting young people across the UK who are embarking on their own journey to success.

Thank you very much.

The Prince's Trust is a registered charity number 1079675, incorporated by Royal Charter.

ISBN 978-1-5272-1404-0

Printed in Great Britain

Alexpress
T: 01932 581460
production@alexpress.co.uk
www.alexpress.co.uk

1st Edition September 2017

cunard.co.uk/millionmakers

At the harbour they gasp at the **size** of the ship;
stowed in a backpack, Charles tightens his grip.

Very soon they will sail, away from the land;
on this very big ship that looks rather *grand*.

As they climb up the gangway,
it feels very high;
"**this is such an *adventure***",
they hear Grandma cry.

On board it looks *magical*,
thinks Charles in his head;
as they meet the smart
bellboys, all dressed in **red**.

A **loud noise** sounds,
the mighty whistle blows;
it's time to set sail…
and off the ship goes.

On the way to their room,
as they start to explore;
Charles **FALLS**
from the backpack
and lands on the floor.

The family
don't notice, they
carry on walking;
they're looking ahead,
as usual they're talking!

A nice man with a smile
picks him up straight away;
he peers at Charles and
says **"You'll be okay"**.

The man with the smile
has a radio transmitter;
he calls out to the crew,
"I need a bear-sitter".

The crew are on stand-by,
they know what to do;
to care for Charles
after what he's
been through.

Paul from the **PLAY ZONE** can bear-sit first;
he gets Charles a drink to quench his thirst.

There are arts and crafts and games to play;
enough toys and activities to fill a whole day.

Paul goes off duty,
he is needed elsewhere;
so a new friend is found
to look after the bear.

It's Lucille from the library,
she chooses a book;
and reads Charles a
story in a *quiet* cosy nook.

At the end of the story,
Lucille has to go;
she hands Charles over
to the **STAR** of a show.

He is so full of energy, he **jitters** and **flitters**;
he can't wait to meet the other bear-sitters.

Daphne the dancer takes
Charles to rehearsals;
she **whirls** and she *twirls*
as she spins round in circles.

Charles loves her costume,
all shiny with glitter;
but he's excited to meet
his next bear-sitter.

It's Carlo the chef, he brings Charles a **cream cake**; and shows him the galley, where his friends cook and bake.

There are platters of seafood
and big plates of meat;
and puddings and cheese
that smells of old feet!

Charles watches the chef
prepare *Afternoon Tea*;
and he dreams about
who his next sitter will be.

Oh wow, it's the Captain
who comes to take charge;
they head to the **bridge**
where the windows are large.

The Captain spots **dolphins**,
who play right ahead;
Charles looks to the left
and sees a **whale** instead!

Good news arrives, the family is sighted;
they are found very quickly and soon reunited!

The Captain explains where Charles has been;
the adventures he's had and who he has seen.

The family is happy to be back with their bear;
from now on they promise to take much more care.

They hatch a plan to keep Charles from harm;
it involves a **bow tie**, they attach to an arm.

Now Charles is secure
and despite being small;
he can go everywhere,
he can no longer fall.

On the days that follow, there is plenty to do;
there are dances and classes and ice carving too.

There are places to visit and sights to explore;
and postcards to send from their **fun days** ashore.

There are pools to swim in and games to play;
there are different activities to do every day.

All too soon the voyage has come to an end,
as the family leave Charles spots an old friend;
it's the nice man with the smile, but who else
can he spy?

It's his bear-sitter friends,
they're all waving *goodbye*.

As they leave the harbour the family agree;

WAY OUT

CHARLES 1

it was a Grand Adventure
that Charles had at sea.

Did you spot all the red bow ties?

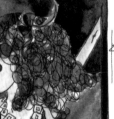

A message from the creators, Ali Webster and Amy Meredith

Q - How does an idea to create a children's book for charity become a reality in just a few months?

A - With the help and support of many internal work colleagues, external suppliers, family members and friends.

We would like to express our sincere thanks and gratitude to every single person who assisted us in making this happen. Every piece of feedback you gave, idea you had, error you spotted, cup of tea you made and line of rhyme you listened to (again and again) has been much appreciated. We know it became a little obsessive at times! Also a very special mention to Ava Hayden (age 8) for helping with the grammar. A very important job indeed.

It's been quite a journey, but we made it. If you are reading this acknowledgment we hope that it's because you have bought a copy of the book. Thank you, and we hope you enjoy it.

Ali and Amy

Avril Taberner, the illustrator's story

From an early age my mother encouraged my creativity and artistic skills, and thanks to her encouragement I went on to university to study textile design. I would spend hours perfecting my project books with illustrations, and despite (sometimes desperate) coaxing by my tutors to be a little rougher with my sketches I soon realised that I had both a perfectionist nature and an absolute passion for drawing. After graduating in 2011 I continued illustrating as a hobby, spending evenings cross stitching and sketching my little fingers away and enjoying my imagination coming to life.

In 2016 I gained the courage to show my work to family and friends. Their positive reactions and support led me to realise that I should pursue my love of drawing into a full-time career. In June 2017 I was approached by Team Cunard Million Makers to see if I would like to illustrate their children's book in aid of The Prince's Trust. Of course I jumped at the chance!

I hope you enjoy my illustrations as much as I enjoyed drawing them – they feel like a part of me now and a part of me is certainly in each one.

Avril x

 AvyTabby Designs   @avytabbydesigns

avytabby.co.uk